THIS JOURNAL BELONGS TO

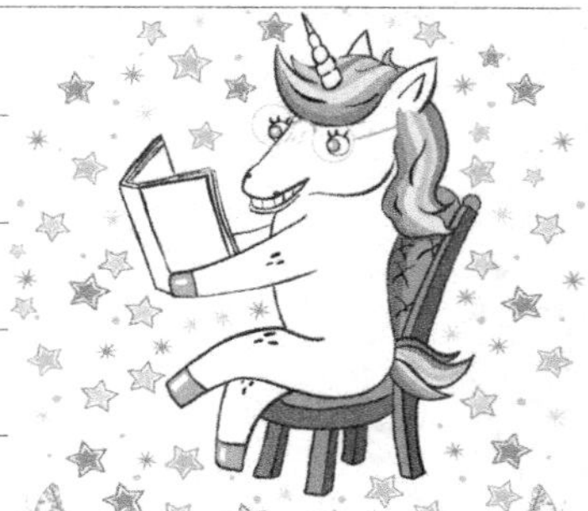

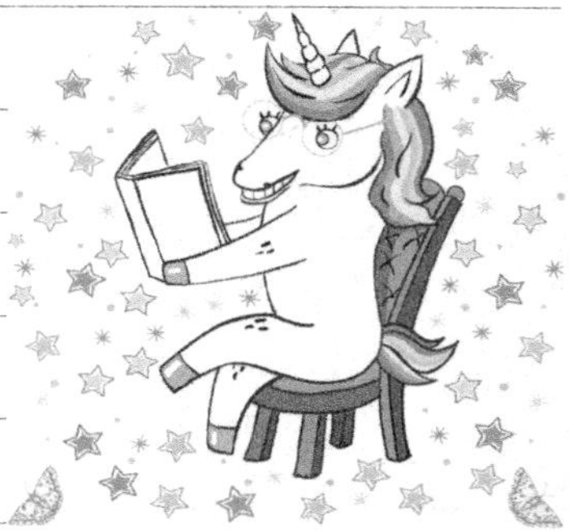

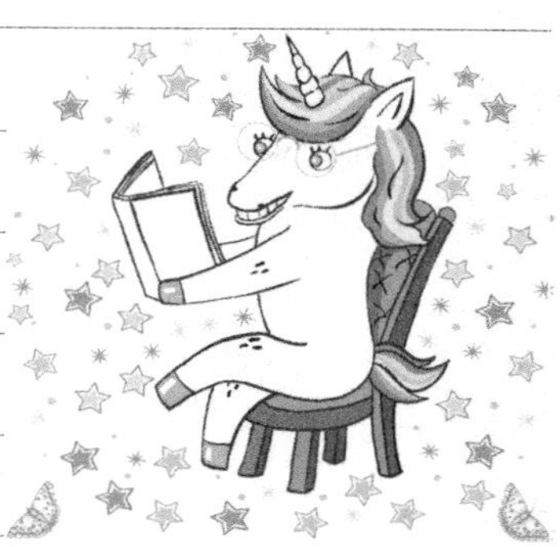

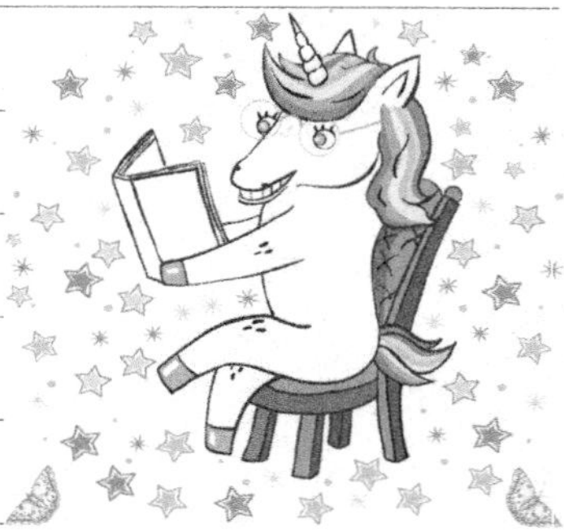

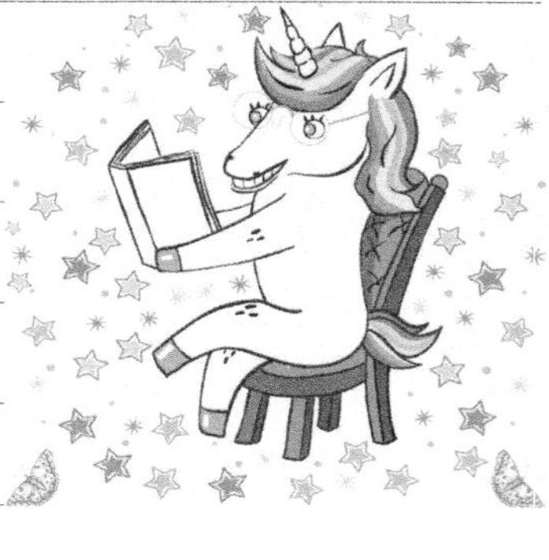

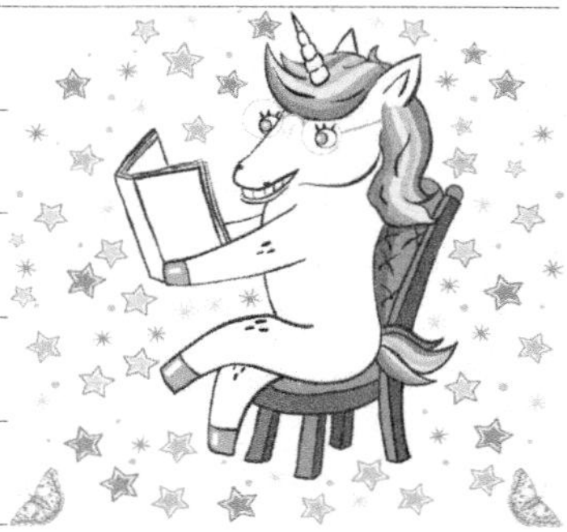

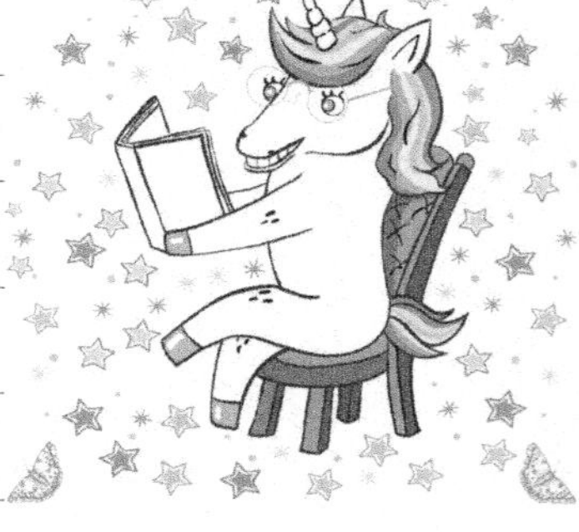

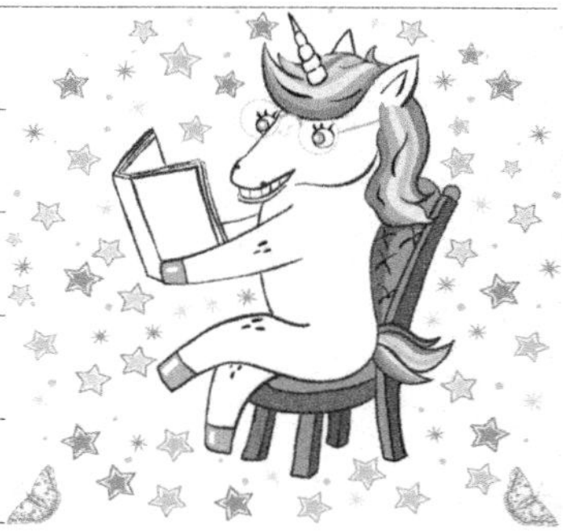

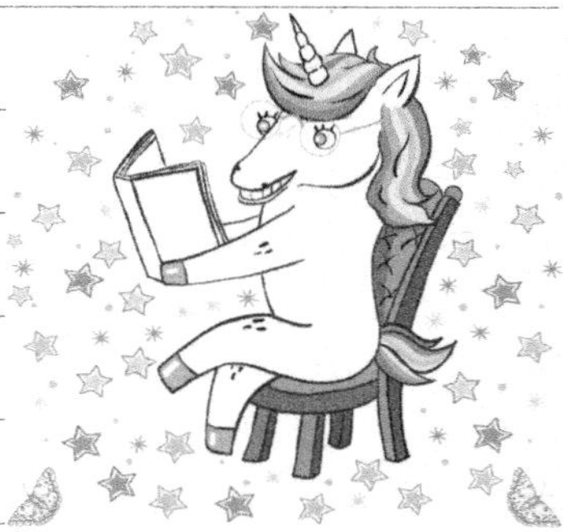

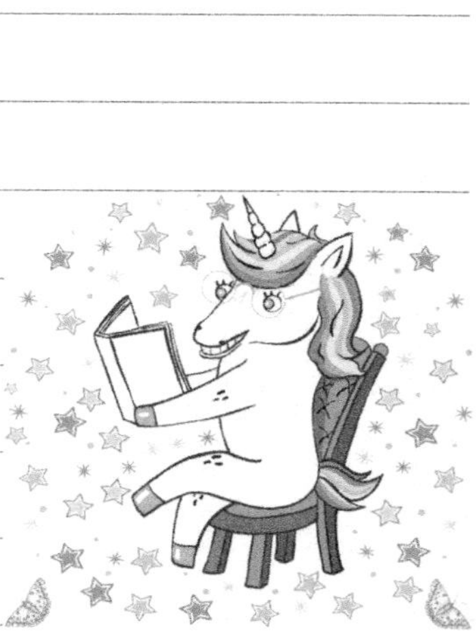

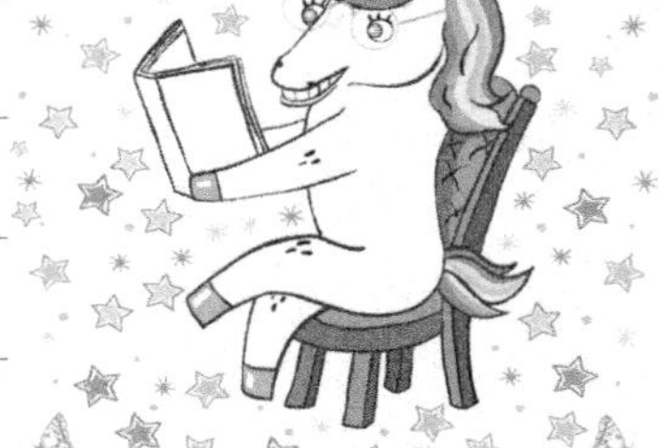

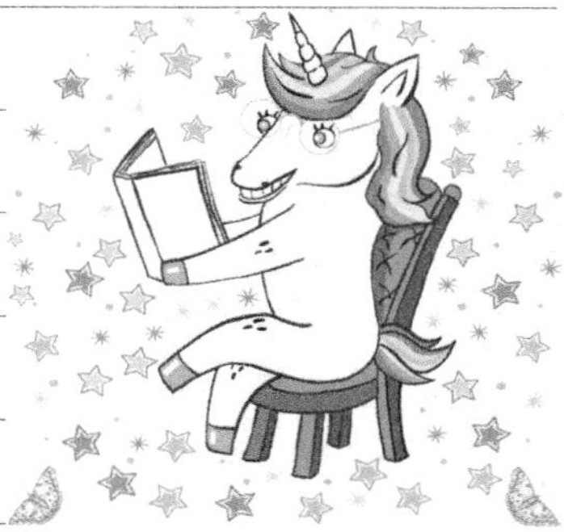

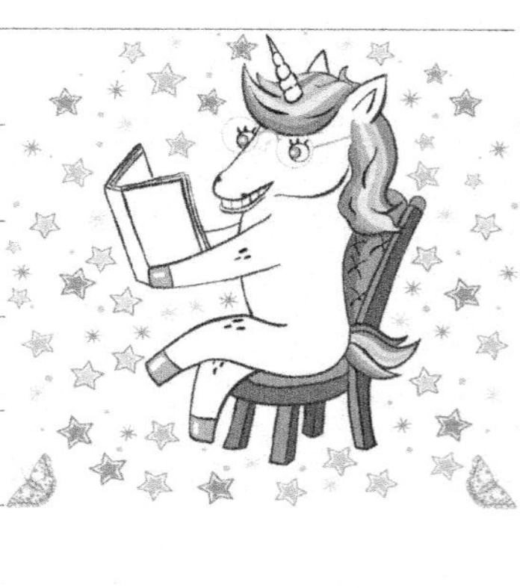

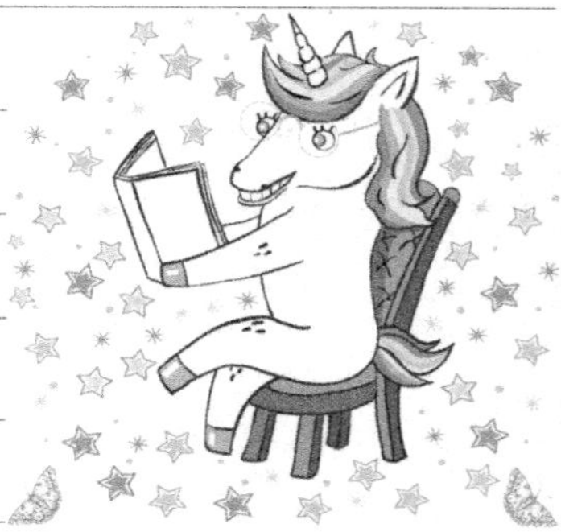

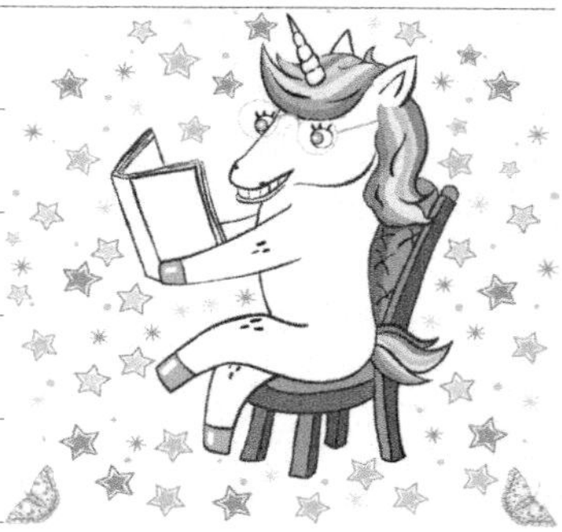

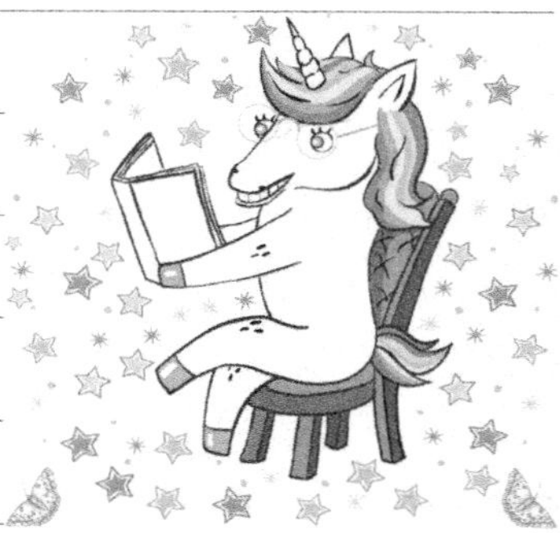

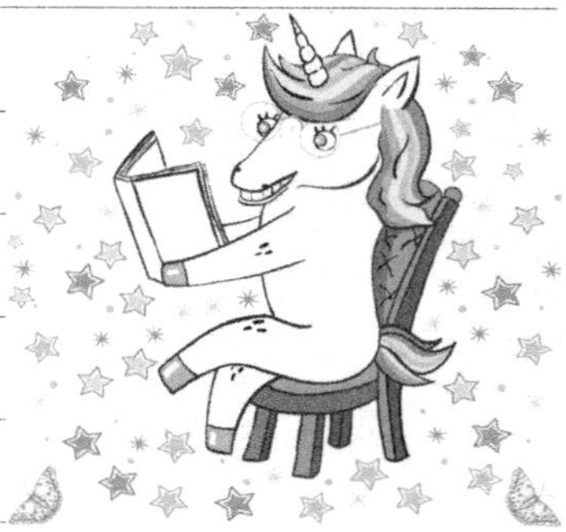

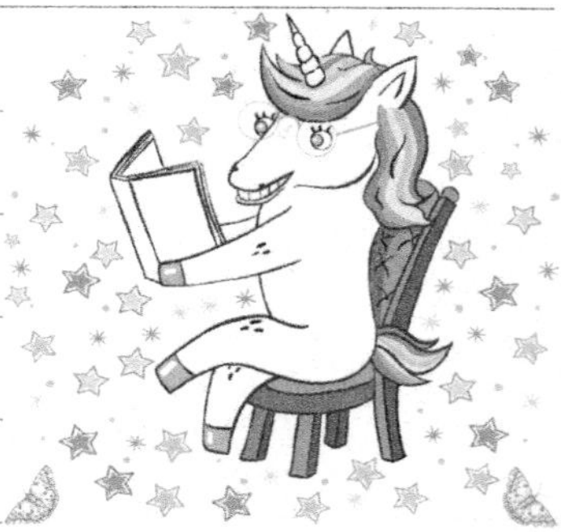

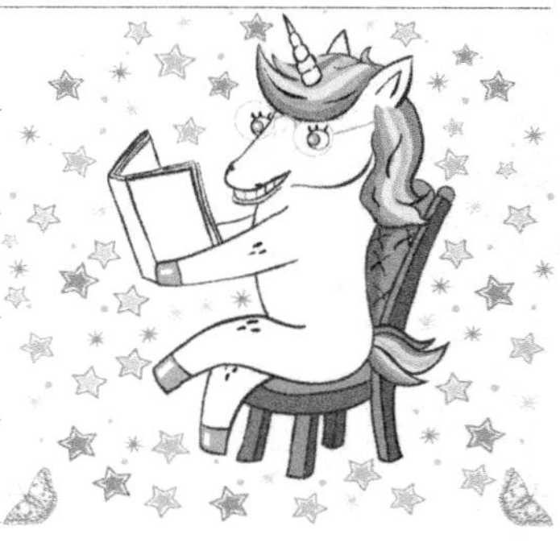

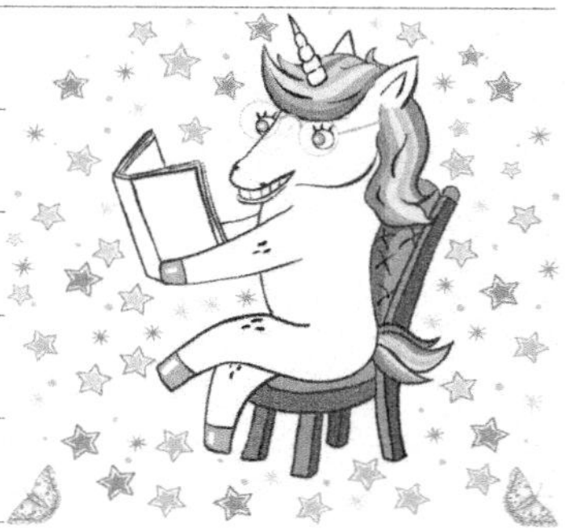

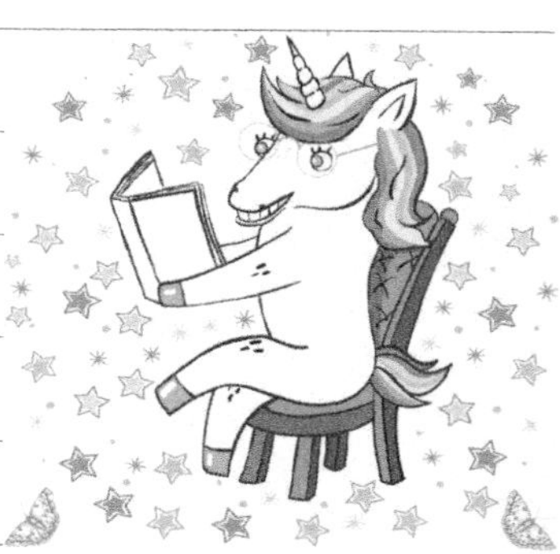

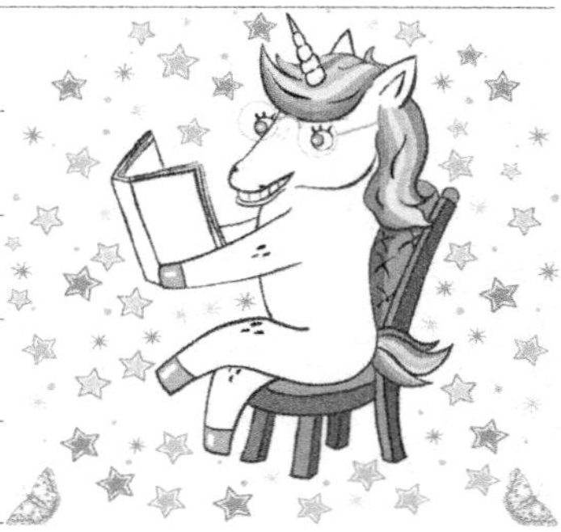

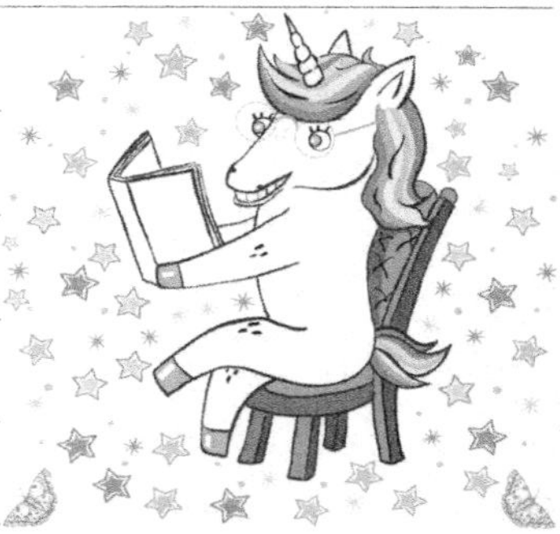

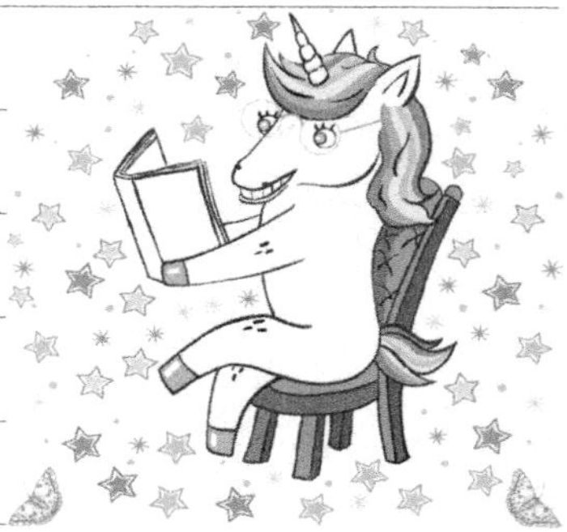

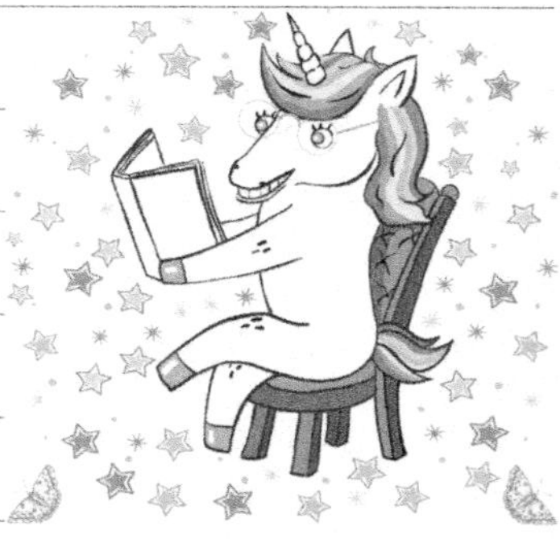

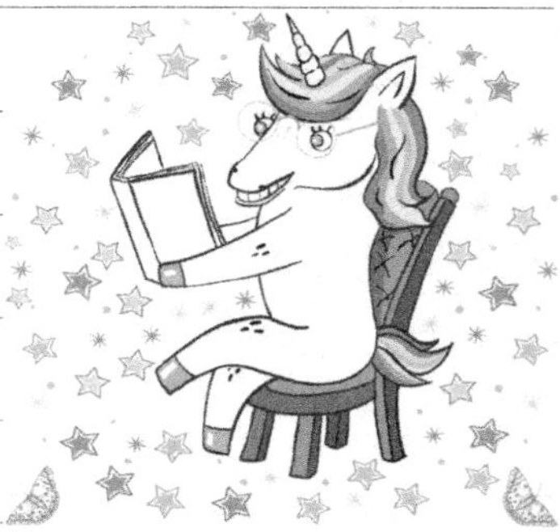

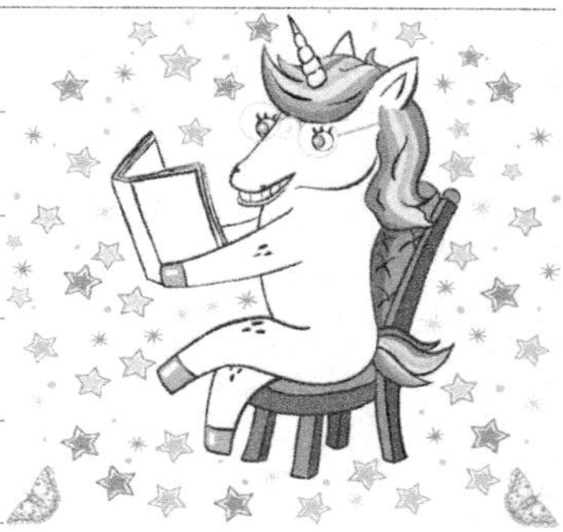

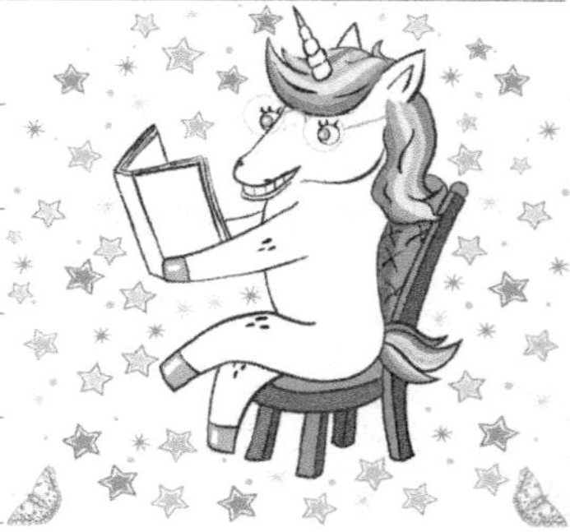

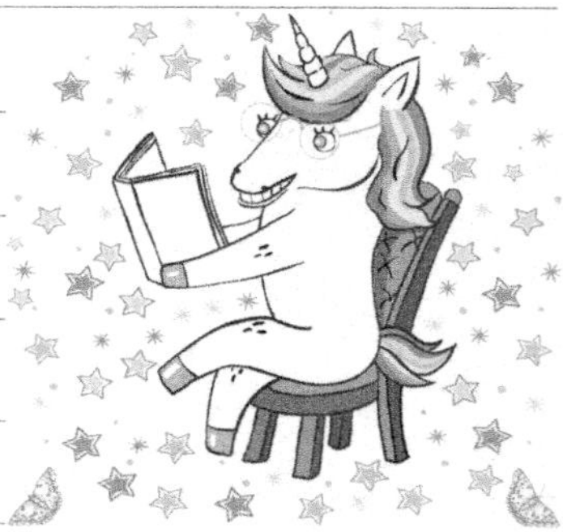

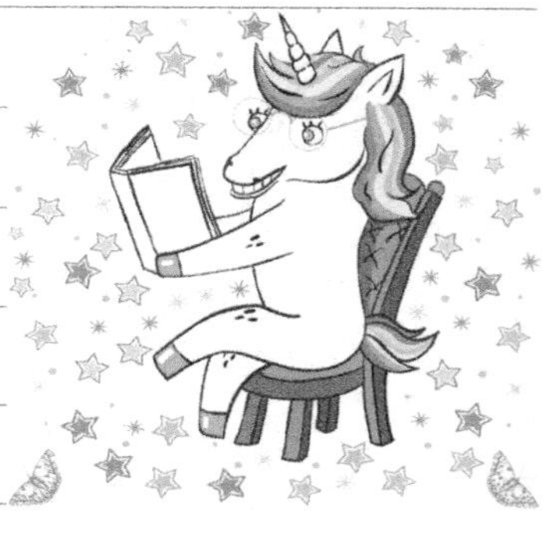

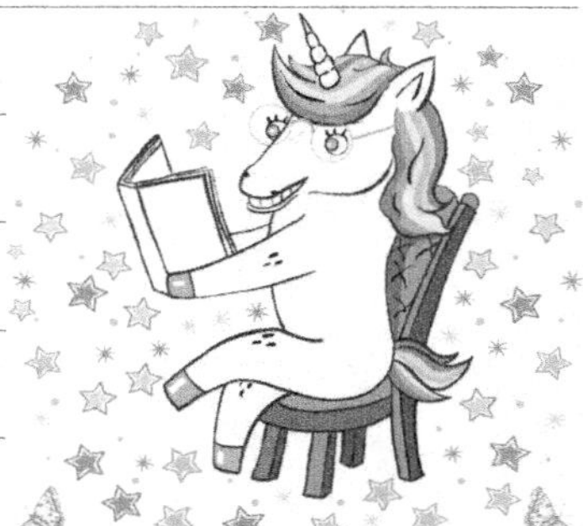

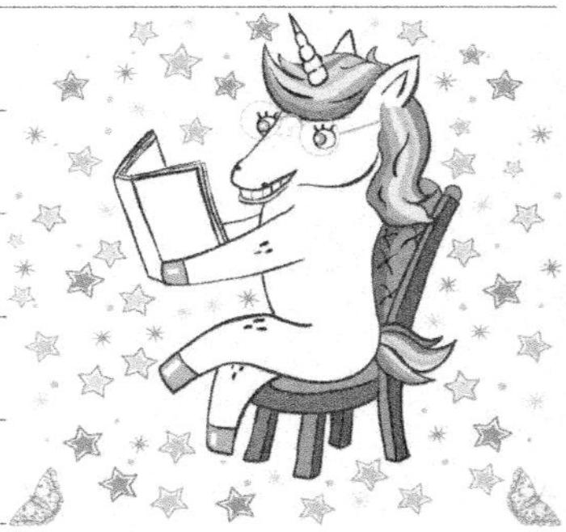

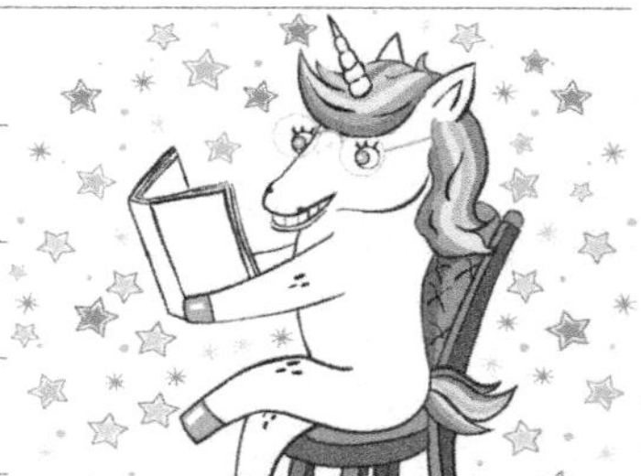

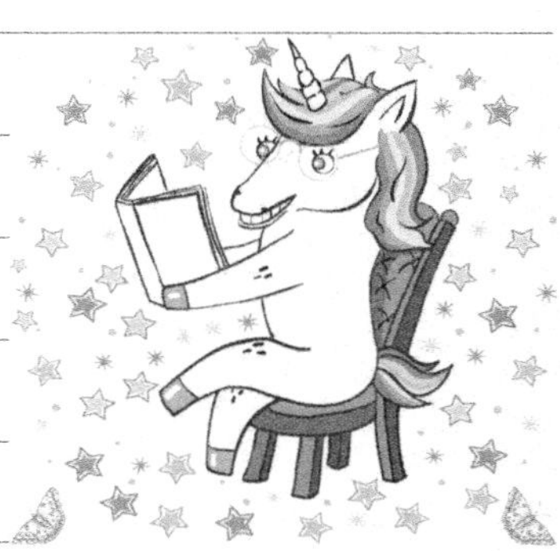

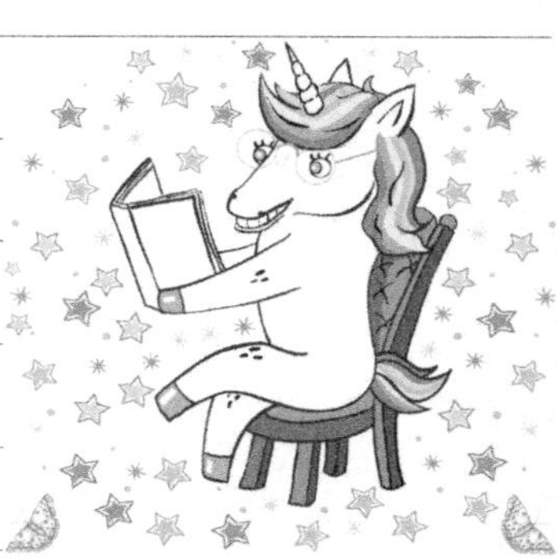

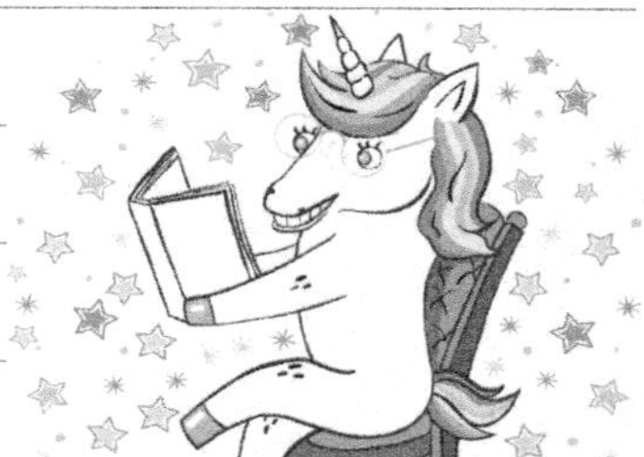

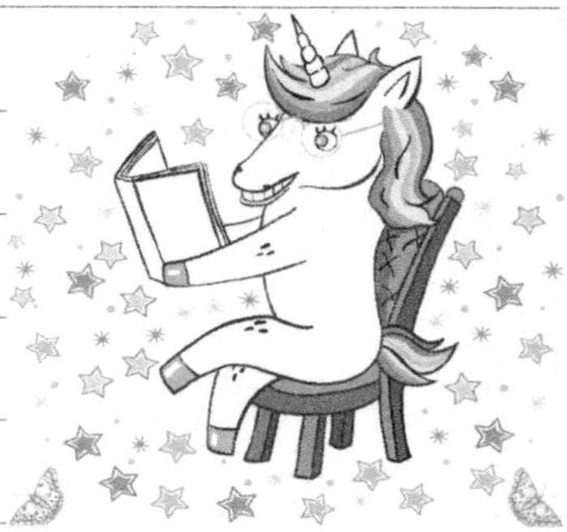

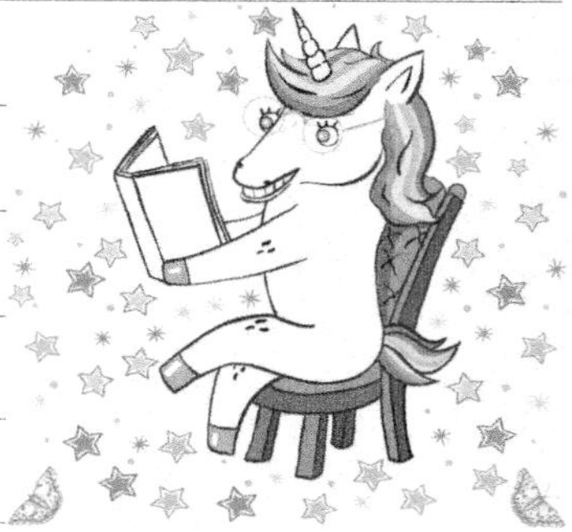

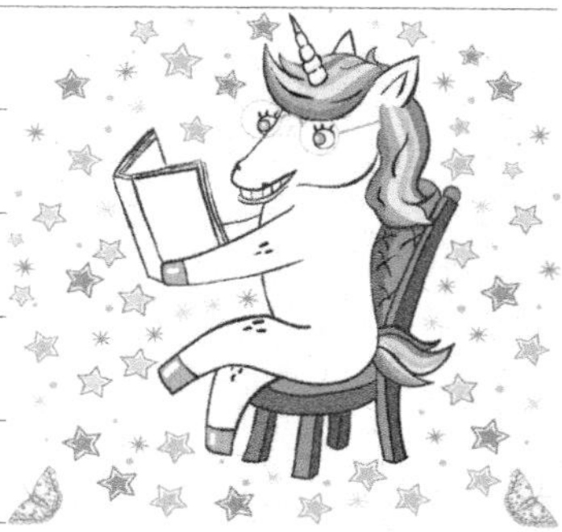

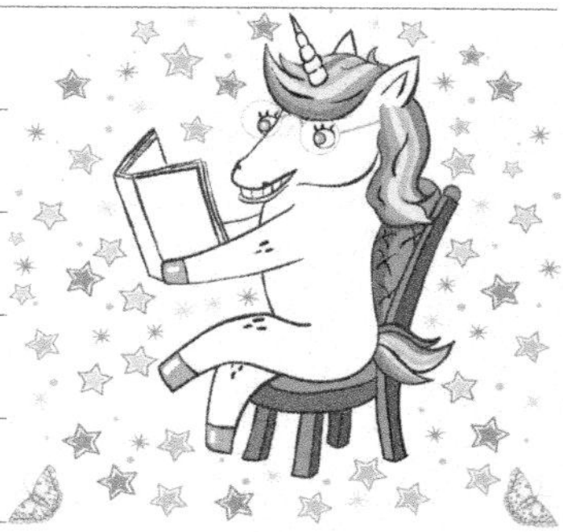

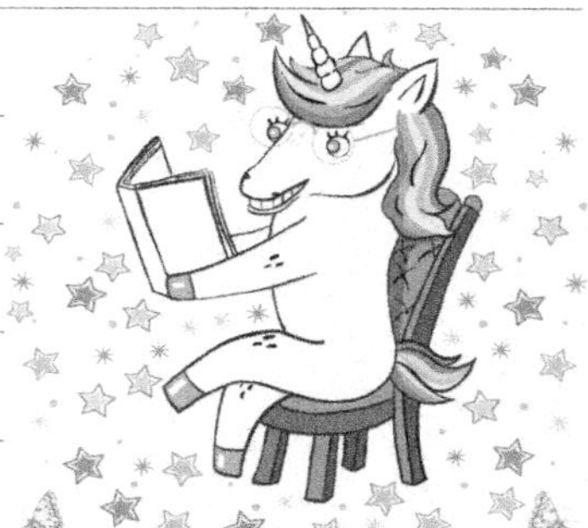

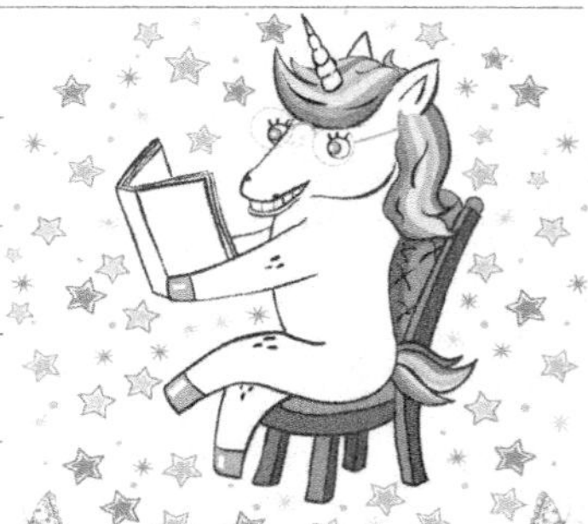

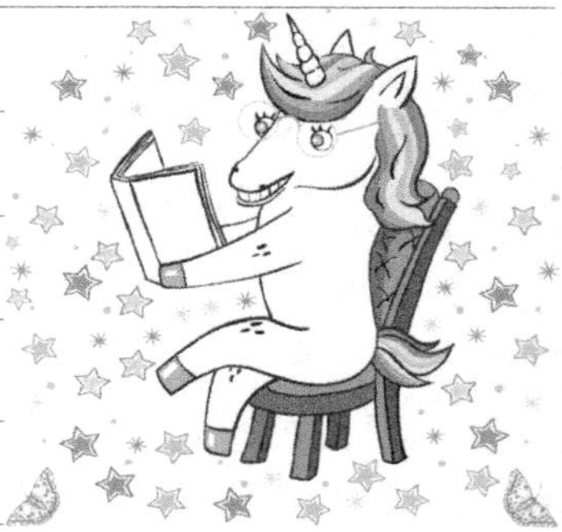

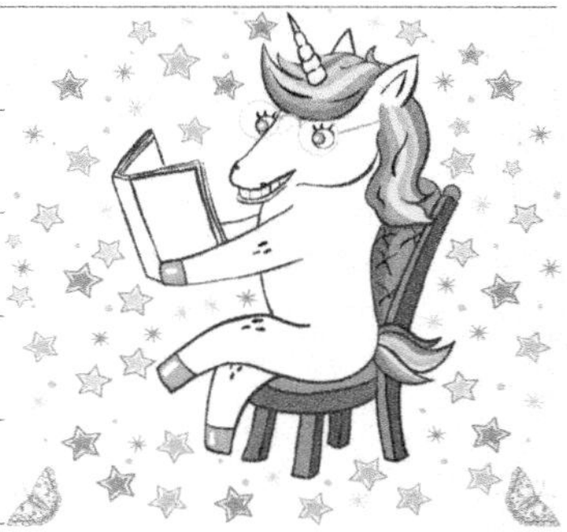

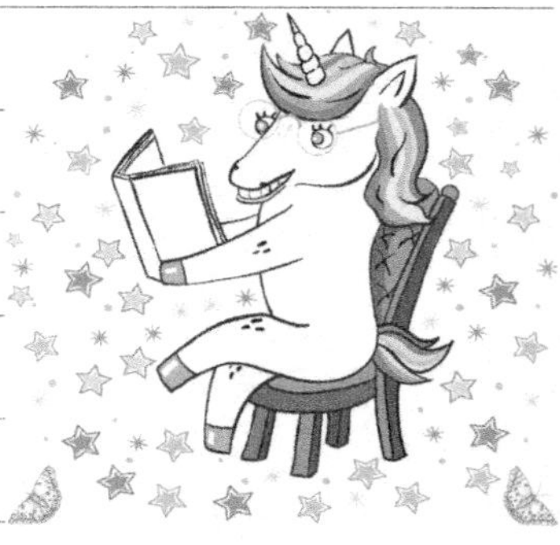

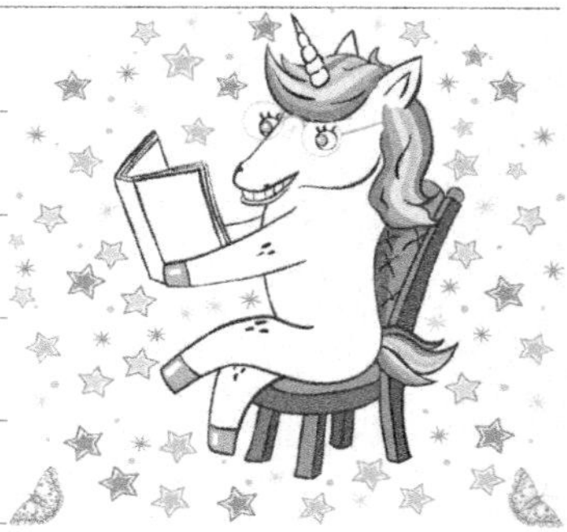

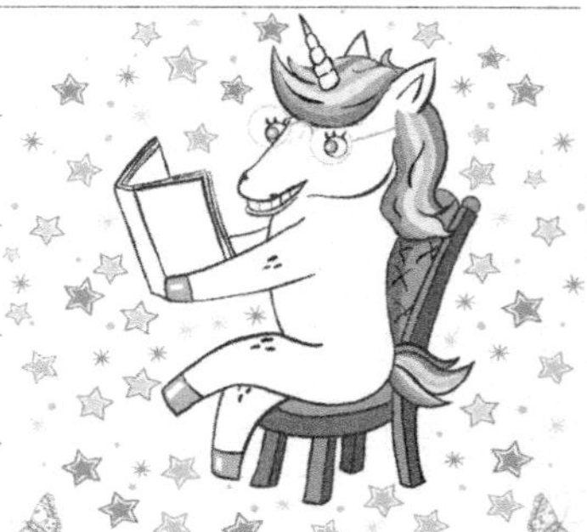

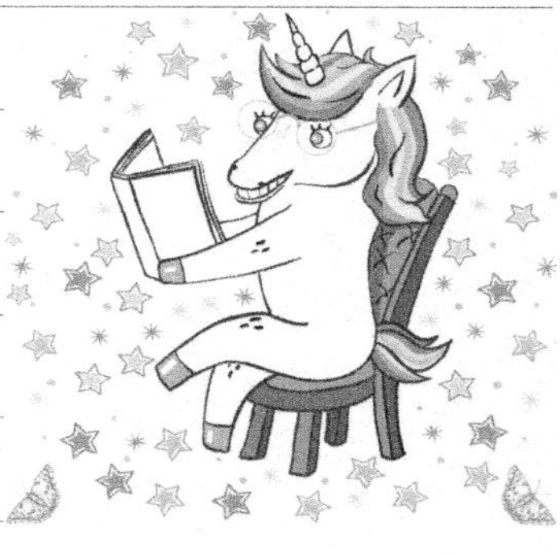

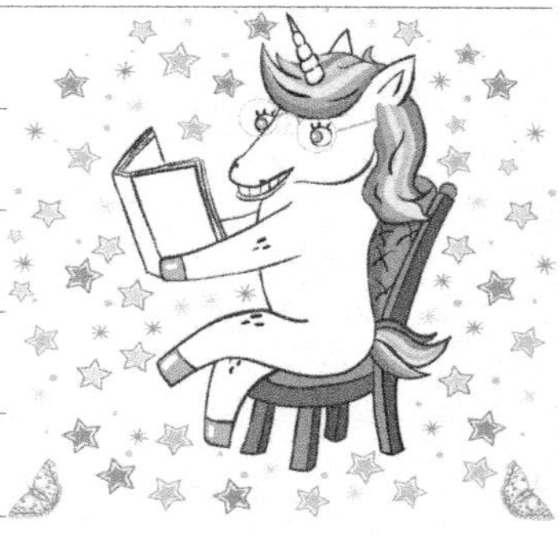

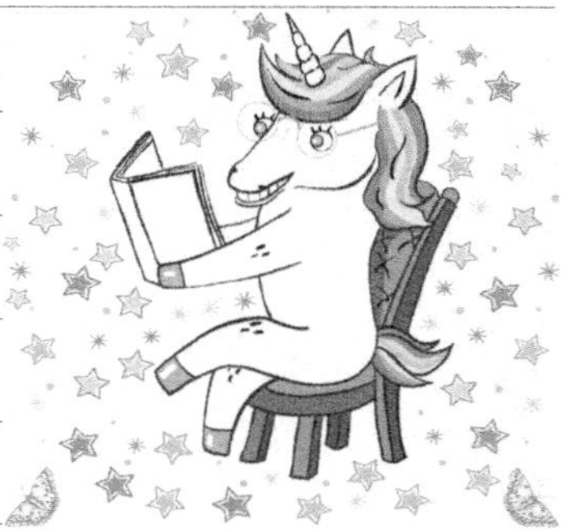

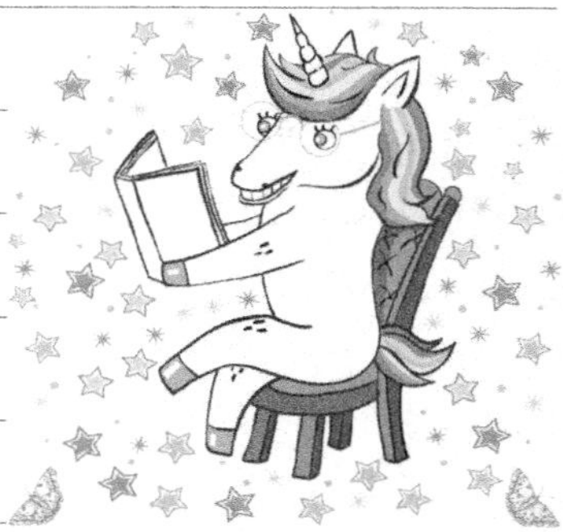

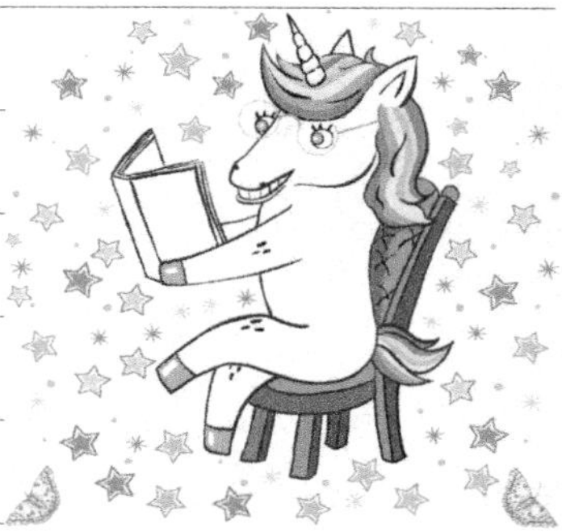

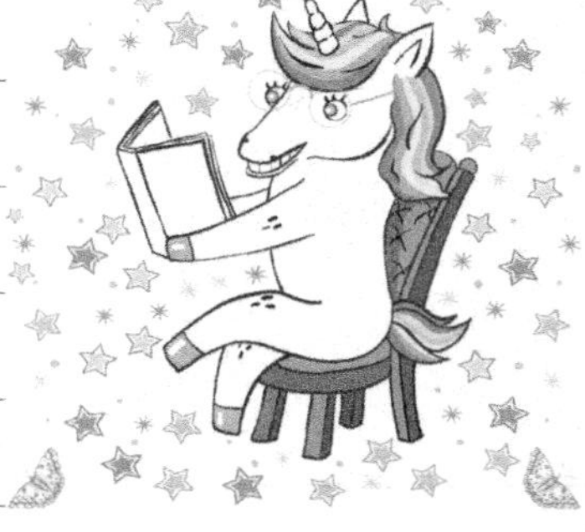

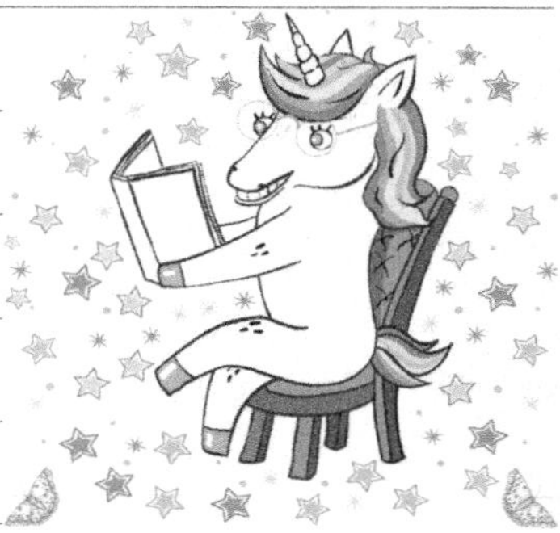

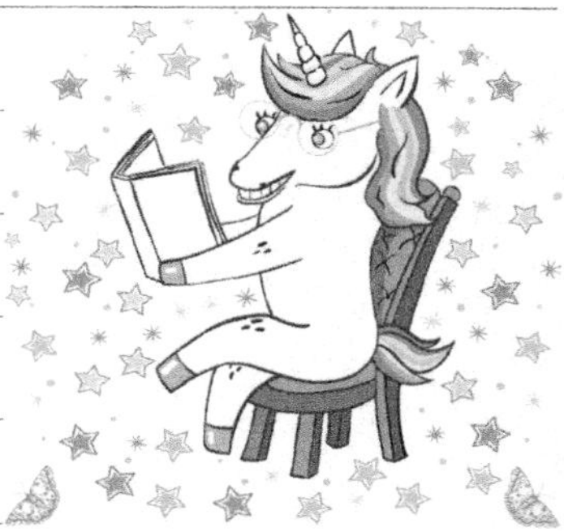

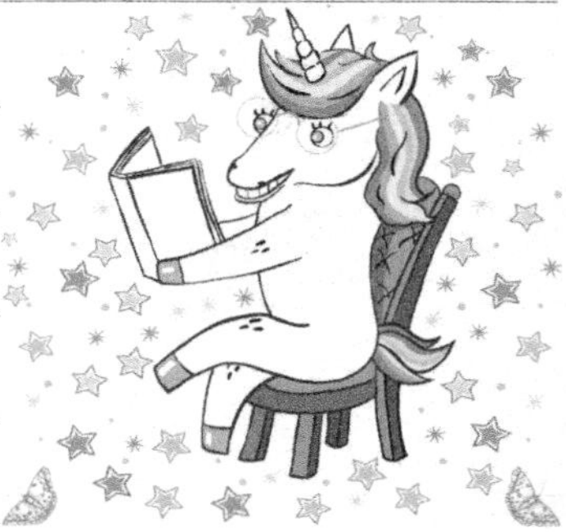

56865144R00066

Made in the USA
Middletown, DE
24 July 2019